MW01140445

Beckoning Lights

MONICA HUGHES

Beckoning Lights

A PANDA BOOK

General
— PAPERBACKS —
Toronto, Canada

A Panda Book, published in 1990 by
General Paperbacks

Published by arrangement with
J.M. LeBel Enterprises

Printed in the United States
Typesetting: Jay Tee Graphics Ltd.

Beckoning Lights

CHAPTER ONE

It all began the night I saw the strange lights...or was it really then? If Jack and I hadn't been telepathic those others would not have overheard us 'talking' about what Jack had seen in the cave. If Mother hadn't died the previous year I would have been at home with her instead on in the Rockies on the field trip with my twin brother Jack and the honour students of Father's Grade Ten class, and then none of it could have happened. So where did it all start?

It was a hot dry July, perfect weather for a field trip in the Rockies, my very first. The previous year Father had taken Jack along as well as his students, but I'd had to stay home because I was a girl. It just didn't seem fair and I'd been miserable. Jack and I had never been far apart, and our telepathy no longer worked.

We'd had it all our lives, and it wasn't until we went to school that we realised that we were different from other kids...we alone could talk inside each other's heads without bothering with words. When we were apart it was like being suddenly struck blind and deaf.

So this year I was along, sharing the back seat of the station wagon with Doug Smalltree and Barry Trevor. I was a bit shy, but straight away Doug set me at ease. I'd seen him around, but of course the High School kids never had anything to do with us Grade Eighters, so I'd never spoken to him before. He was a Stoney Indian, and in his blue jeans and moccasins, rawhide jacket and leather thong tied round his head to keep his straight black hair out of his eyes, he really looked at home in the bush. He had a way of speaking, slow and soft, that made me feel comfortable right away.

Barry was completely different. He was thin and blond all over, skin, hair, eyes, as if he'd never been out of doors before. His voice was sharp and a bit too high, and the whole trip he picked at having to have a girl tag along. Father never noticed. He hummed snatches of operatic marches as he drove. About half of him was concentrating on the highway, which was full of 'sorry you've been inconvenienced' notices, where road crews were still patching up the spring potholes and frost heaves. The other half of him was probably back in the school science lab mulling over the experiment he'd had to abandon when the school had closed for the summer.

Doug cut through Barry's snide remarks and began to tell me about the geology of the countryside. He talked about it being once a coral sea, then a tropical swamp, before the land lifted and turned it into the grassland, forests and mountains of today. His explanations lasted us right up to the track which turned north off the highway and led up into the mountains where we were to spend our week.

The road was dusty and unused, with sharp stones sticking up and great ruts where the spring rains had washed out the soil. Flowers and grass grew hood-high in the centre of the track. It felt like bull-dozing through the Amazon jungle, as Father coaxed the station wagon along.

"Nobody could have been here in years!" Barry exclaimed.

"A month maybe," Doug suggested. "See, only a few woody plants broke as we went by. The others just sprang up again."

I wriggled around to look. He was right. We were in a sea of grass and flowers. Father carefully eased the car off the track and parked among the bushes and we all got out and stretched.

"Up there is a fire-tower." Father pointed, "You can just see the top of it from here."

We craned up at the rocky slope on our right and saw a path hairpinning dizzily to and from to the summit. I caught the gleam of sun on metal, blinding for a second. The heat bounced off the hot rock into our faces, and the dark wood below the mountain began to look very good.

We began to load up. Jack helped me with my knapsack harness and then strapped my sleeping bag on top. I could feel my knees beginning to bend, but I was bound and determined to keep up with the boys. "I've got a spare hand," I volunteered with a tight grin, but Jack just gave me one of his looks and pointed me along the trail.

I staggered off and for the next half hour concentrated on keeping my feet. The trail wound casually across a densely wooded valley that lay like a dark stream between the hot bare mountains. The footing was good, pine needles and moss, and the spruces and lodge-pole pines gave a most welcome shade. Boy, it was hot! Way over on my left I could hear the enticing sound of running water. I licked my dry lips and plodded on. The trail began to climb and the sun sent

4

dazzling shafts of light through the thinning trees. I staggered when the sun suddenly blinded me, and felt Father's hand under my arm.

"Just another hundred yards. You're doing fine, Julia." His long legs loped past me, his back bent by two tents and a bedroll. By the time I'd got my breath and wiped the sweat out of my eyes he had cleared a patch of grass on the little plateau he'd picked for our camp. He looked cool and relaxed, his eyes behind their horn-rimmed glasses half-shut against the glare, his pipe clamped between his teeth. Thankfully I dumped my load and sat on it, black spots dancing in front of my eyes.

Jack and the others came up the trail. "You're as red as a beet," Barry informed me, but I noticed that he was panting. Doug looked relaxed and cool. He never seemed to hurry, but he always got things done.

Father left Jack and me to pitch the tents. We were a good team and it certainly helped knowing what the other person was going to do next, without having to waste a lot of words and breath over it. Father and Barry and Doug went back down the trail to bring back the food and the geological gear. I could have laughed out loud at the expression on Barry's face, but I decided that one stinker on the expedition was enough, so I tactfully turned my back and began to fuss with the tent so that he couldn't see my grin.

We got the tents up in record time. It was fun working with Jack, like being one person with four hands. We grinned at each other and then Jack grew serious. "Look, Jule..."

"I know. We'll have to be careful that Barry and Doug don't find out about our telepathy. It'll be difficult, living with them for a whole week."

"Well, if we slip up now and then we can cover it up, but let's try to remember not to mind-read unless we're alone."

"Right. Let's get the wood, shall we?"

We dropped down off the plateau to the edge of the trees and began to collect handfuls of small wood and bark for kindling. Then Jack found a fallen pine-tree. At first we thought it had been struck by lightning, but there were no char marks and the splintered end was clean and white.

"That's funny. I've never seen a tree like that."

"It looks as if an elephant had gone by." Jack fingered the sharp, still resinous edges of the break. "Look, Jule! See that tree top, way up there. It's been splintered in just the same way."

"A flying elephant, doubtless."

He punched me in a friendly fashion and between

us we managed to drag the whole tree up the campsite and started sawing it into manageable lengths. By the time the others staggered up the trail for the second time we had made a grand fireplace with stones on a natural granite slab and had a pile of wood neatly beside it.

This time Barry looked really beat and I felt sorry for him. Even Father was puffed and he'd put his pipe in his pocket. Doug was as unruffled as ever, though he'd shed his rawhide jacket.

"I'll have tea in a minute, if you'll show me where to get water," I volunteered.

Father pointed to the south end of the plateau. "It was good water when I was up here three years ago, but we'll drink it boiled until we've had a chance to ask the fire-watcher if it's still safe. If you're dying for a cold drink you must use the purification tablets, one to a mug. Don't cheat. We don't want stomach upsets."

I dug out the kettle and ran down the grassy slope. There it was, a small stream coming down fast and cool from the mountain above us. The bottom was pebbly and it was easy to get a kettleful of clean water. By the time I got back Doug had a small hot fire going in the new fireplace.

He took the kettle from me with a grin. "It's a good

fireplace. Not too large and the draught is just right.''

I found myself grinning happily back and went to find teabags and the big pot and our mugs. The tea tasted special, on the grass by the fire, with a little breeze coming down the pass between the mountain behind us and the one to the south. It didn't stir the spruces in the valley below, but up on the plateau it cooled us off beautifully.

Afterwards I felt so full of energy I went into our tent and arranged everything properly. We'd brought two nine by twelve tents, one for the three boys, the other for Father and me, the extra space in ours for stowing supplies. I blew up the air-mattresses and laid out the sleeping bags at right angles to each other with Father's special equipment box safely in the corner. Against the other tent wall I arranged cans and freeze-dried packets of food, so that I wouldn't have to hunt around if we were late and tired and needing a meal. By the time I was finished it was half-past six and the shadows outside were growing long.

I got out the hamburger meat and buns and the salad and watermelon that we'd brought up in the big cooler and began to get supper organized. The cooler itself we'd left back in the station wagon, full of cans of pop. It was far too heavy to carry. Doug made up the fire for me, and I fried the hamburgers brown and juicy.

I really can cook. Mother taught me before she got sick.

It was when we had got to the watermelon stage and were sitting in a row seeing how far we could spit the seeds that I first saw it. I was looking south towards the far mountain, past the stream and the scree-covered saddle that separated us from it. The sun was low, glancing across the crags, lighting up bright points here and there. I thought I was seeing things. I blinked and shaded my eyes and looked again. It was still there, a great gash in the mountainside, a dark shadow against the sunlit rock.

"Do look, everyone! Over there."

"What is it? Did a gopher scare you?" Barry laughed.

"A cave!" Jack was the first to see it. "Dad, you never told us about a cave."

"I've never seen one." Father unwound his long legs and brought the binoculars out of the tent. "It's darned odd. I've camped up here dozens of times. I could have sworn that there was nothing..."

"A real cave! And I found it!"

"Let's take a bearing on it and we'll be sure of finding it again tomorrow." Barry's voice was so eager I knew he was hoping for fabulous finds of gold or jade or something.

"Why not? We'll explore it in the morning." Father

fished his compass out of his pocket and took a careful bearing. "A point south of south-south-west. The elevation we'll just have to guess at right now."

"It won't be that hard to find, Dad. I mean, just look at it." As I waved my arm the sun dipped behind the saddle, and as if I had pulled a switch the tell-tale shadow of the cave went out. There was nothing to see at all. The rock face looked completely blank. It was so sudden that I think we all shouted in surprise.

"It really is remarkable." Father squinted through the binoculars again. "Can't make out a sign of it. Here, you fellows, see if you can still spot it. I'm going to help our cook with the dishes."

It was really only a couple of bowls, the mugs and the greasy frying pan, but I was glad of the chance to have Father to myself for a little while.

"Enjoying yourself?" he asked, as he rinsed out the mugs. I didn't answer for a minute, struggling to scrub out the pan with sand from the edge of the stream. It wasn't too satisfactory. Another time I'd boil water.

"Thanks, Dad, it's great," I said at last. "But are you really sure it'll be all right if I come with you guys on your serious field trips? I can always stay in camp."

"I thought that was all decided." He looked amazed. I didn't think he'd noticed the way Barry was needling me.

"Maybe Doug and Barry will get bored having a younger girl tag along all the time," I suggested.

"I really don't see why. Being a girl is not some sort of plague."

I sighed. "It is sometimes. It really isn't fair. If I couldn't have been a boy why couldn't I have been spectacularly beautiful, with no zits and with wavy hair and long eyelashes like Jack. After all he doesn't *need* them."

"Perhaps there's something very special on your straight-hair chromosome that you wouldn't want to be without."

"I can't think what. There's nothing special about me. I'm overweight and I'm not as smart as Jack, and I'm scared of so many stupid things, like being shut in closets or elevators and being alone."

"Does that still bother you, Julia? I thought you'd grown out of it."

"Maybe it's not as bad as it used to be. Maybe I'm just used to it. Oh, well, I suppose we'd better get back to the others. This pan is as clean as it's ever going to be."

"I'm glad you're here, Julia. Apart from your bright and shining face you're a better cook than I am."

I laughed and felt better, though I still didn't feel too happy about horning in on the field trips. On the other hand, I certainly didn't want to be left alone all day while the others went off exploring.

As soon as the sun went down it grew rapidly cooler, and we turned in early in spite of protests from Barry. I don't know what sort of night life he'd been expecting up in the mountains.

"The sun will be shining into our tents before five," Doug pointed out. "Better we sleep when it's dark and get up with the sun." Barry was speechless. The idea of getting up before five shook him even more than going to bed before ten.

I snuggled into my sleeping bag. The air mattress was exactly firm enough and the down filling of my bag was warm and light. A breeze scented with evergreen and meadow-sweet drifted in through the door. The flaps were rolled back and through the netting I could see the stars flickering. Tomorrow we would explore my cave. I went to sleep feeling wonderfully happy.

I woke all at once. My skin was tight and prickly all over, like the time I'd stood in the field of the electrostatic machine at the science fair. My short straight hair had stood up on end and my skin had crawled like this...but that day at the fair I hadn't felt so afraid.

What was the matter? I peered at my watch in the dim moonlight. Two in the morning. *Two*...I almost decided to duck back into the warmth of my sleeping bag. It was probably just the effects of a bad dream...too much watermelon. But something urged me out of bed, towards the tent door.

It all looked very peaceful out there. There was a faint pre-dawn glow in the north-eastern sky and the stars over there had lost some of their brilliance. Below me the forest was inky black, and Lookout Mountain was a dark silhouette against the sky.

I was on my way back to bed when I saw the light out of the corner of my eye. I blinked and looked again. What on earth? A meteor? Too close and bright. An airplane? Too low. My eyes gradually made out the outline and I knew, with a sudden swoop of terror, that it could be neither.

Its oval shape hovered over the dark valley. As I watched, white and green lights blinked on around the perimeter like a bright necklace. Like a bird of prey it hovered silently above the forest, and I knelt on the cold floor of the tent, shivering, afraid to move or call for help.

Suppose it...they...heard me, or saw me move. What did they want? What were they doing out there? My knees ached and I wondered how long I had been watching. I took a cautious look at my watch. Still two o'clock. Stupid! I must have forgotten to wind it. But I hadn't. I remembered distinctly.

I stared till my eyes watered, kneeling at the tent door, clutching at the rolled back tent flaps with hands that were ice-cold and yet sweaty. Quite suddenly the lights, which had risen almost imperceptibly until they were level with my eyes, began to revolve rapidly. I froze. I think I even stopped breathing.

There was a faint humming noise that rose in pitch to an almost unbearable whine, and the thing rose into the air and came directly towards me. An enormous shadow passed over the tent, blotting out the stars.

I crouched on the cold tent floor with my eyes shut, my hands over the back of my neck, waiting for I don't know what blow to fall. I was too scared to move or even to cry out.

CHAPTER TWO

"Jule, don't be scared." Jack's voice was clear and calming inside my mind. It was almost as if he were right inside the tent with me. "Jule, are you all right?"

I found I could move and think again. I sat up slowly and looked out of the tent door. The valley was dark and peaceful. And empty. I let my breath out on a long shaky sigh. "I *think* so," I told him back.

"What was it? A bad dream?"

I sent him a mental picture of what I'd seen and got back a feeling of disbelief. "Like in *flying saucer*? Jule, you're kidding me...okay, okay. I know you're not. It's just...well, I'll take a look around. You go back to bed. I can tell you're freezing."

"Be careful, Jacko. Don't let them see you, if they're still around."

His reckless laughter rang in my mind. To Jack danger was like the relish on the hamburger. That way we were completely opposites. I crept past the sleeping lump that was Father and climbed into my sleeping bag. I was still trying to warm my icy toes with an equally icy hand when Jack's voice came back inside my mind.

"Nothing to be seen, Jule. Go to sleep. We'll talk about it in the morning."

I knew I'd never be able to get to sleep again in a million years. I was still jittery with the memory of that huge thing. And I was freezing. I popped my cold nose inside the sleeping bag to warm it up, and when I took it out again the sun was streaming into the tent. I stretched and yawned and looked at my watch. A bit after five...And I thought: my watch is working again. And I remembered. The circle of lights. The enormous shadow. Had it all been a dream?

I got up quietly and dressed in jeans and a shirt, and crept out to do some sketchy washing in the ice-cold stream. I filled the kettle while I was there and a pot for the porridge. Doug was up and had the fire going by the time I got back. I sent out an exploratory thought to Jack, but his mind was blank to me. He must still be asleep, I thought, and set to work on breakfast. I was determined to be the best cook the camp had ever had.

In half an hour porridge and coffee were keeping hot at the edge of the fire, a pound of bacon was sizzling in the pan, and I was cutting and buttering a huge plateful of bread. The appetizing smells got to Father and Jack and Barry, and, one by one, they poked their heads out, blinking and yawning.

"Six-fifteen." Father looked at his watch. "You really stole a march on us this time, Julia."

"Six-fifteen? It's only a quarter to six."

"No. You're slow. This watch is never wrong."

I stared down at my watch while the others washed and dressed. My watch had lost a half hour, some time in the middle of the night, while I'd crouched on the tent floor, waiting and watching. It had been real. It wasn't a dream. Only it had seemed longer than half an hour. Much longer.

By seven the dishes were done, the sleeping bags were airing in the sun, and we were ready to go. We planned to make our way around the shoulder of 'our' mountain, looking for interesting formations and specimens, and then cross over to the twin peak to the south and climb along its face until we came upon the cave. It was only a couple of kilometres from mountain side to side, but it took us more than two hours, what with hammering at likely-looking rocks, learned discussions about folds and anticlines, most of it over my head, and some sketchy map-making.

Jack was in his element, plying Doug and Father with questions, but somehow I couldn't get excited. My mind kept going back to the night before. I found a big reddish stone among the scree at the edge of the saddle. Father said it was jasper and that he'd have it polished to make a paper-weight for me, but even then I couldn't get thrilled. I had a flat heavy before-thunder feeling in my stomach and I didn't know why.

We scrambled along the steep flank of the southern mountain, looking for my cave. It was funny. It seemed more unreal to me than the lights...I wasn't even sure that I'd really seen it. Father stopped and dug out the compass. He sighted on our camp, clear across the slope of scree. I could even see the coffee pot catching the sun on its polished surface.

"A point north of north-north-east," Father muttered. He walked on and took another sighting. "It must be around here."

"I think it was higher up, Mr. Christie," Barry said.

"Could be. Let's string out, about ten yards apart, up the slope. Then we can't miss it."

Even following Father's suggestion we nearly did. It was the most secret cave I ever saw. Jack only found it by nearly falling in from above. When we all scrambled up to where he was we could see why. The western wall of the entrance almost overlapped the eastern wall. You could walk right by and swear that it was all smooth rock. From the other direction it looked like a deep crack, nothing more. The tell-tale shadow for those few moments at sunset was the only key to the cave.

Father got out his flashlight. I could see his eyes gleam behind his glasses and I knew he was every bit as excited as the boys. "Hold on, fellows. We're not equipped for cave exploring. We don't even have any rope. If this turns out to be a really big cave system we'll just have to come back another time. Now let me go first and look around."

He plunged into the cleft and the shadows swallowed him up. We couldn't hear a thing and after a bit I began to get worried, but just then he popped out again into the sunlight, blinking and shading his eyes. "Nothing too big, I'm afraid. Just a perfectly ordinary cave. Funny smell, but the air doesn't seem to have done me any harm, so let's go."

Barry and Doug plunged into the cave with Jack and me close behind. There was just a muddle of alternate shadow and glare as we all moved our flashlights to and from over the walls and ceiling. When we'd calmed down and kept our flashlights still we could see better.

It was quite a deep cave, sloping gently downward into darkness. Near the entrance the floor was covered with sand and loose stones, but further in it was rock. There was an odd smell, bitter-sweet, different. It grew stronger as we moved forward towards the far wall. Was that it? Just a dead end?

I think we all saw the crack in the back wall at the same instant. There was a concerted rush forward. The boys shouted, their voices tossed to and fro by the echoes, changed, unfamiliar. It was a big cave, but I was beginning to get that breathless shut-in feeling. I wanted to get out. Their voices seemed to be coming from a long way away.

"No good...it's far too narrow. I can't even get my shoulders in." That was Barry.

"Me neither," Doug answered.

"Let me have a go. I'll bet I can do it." Jack's voice was eager and he pushed past the other two and slipped like an eel into the crevice. Almost at once he was out of sight. "Jack, don't! Come back." My voice sounded like a stranger's, high and despairing.

Behind me Father exclaimed, "Jack, no. Not alone." But Jack couldn't hear, and gulping, I pushed myself into the uninviting darkness and reached out to grab Jack's shoulder. He hadn't got far and almost at once my fingers felt the material of his jean jacket. At once, without meaning to at all, I was inside his mind, feeling what he felt. I could sense the weight of the mountain, above us, around us, great masses of rock pressing on shoulders, ribs, thighs.

I let go and backed out of the crack and ran for the entrance of the cave. Outside my knees gave way and I sat down on the blazing rock, trying to steady my shaky breath, trying to calm down before the others came out and saw me. I was so angry with myself I could have cried. I could just hear Barry's taunts: just like a girl, scared of the dark! I pressed my hands together and willed myself back to calmness.

They erupted out of the cave in an excited bunch. "Julia, you should have *seen* it..." Jack began and then stopped.

"Julia, dear, what *is* the matter? You're as white as a sheet." Father put his arm around me and for a horrible moment I thought I might actually start crying.

I swallowed and managed to say quite normally, "I'm fine, thanks. I just felt sick for a moment. It was a bit stuffy in there."

Jack flashed me a sorry-and-we'll-talk-when-we're-alone thought. Then he turned to the others, his eyes sparkling. "Gosh, it was great. Too bad you couldn't squeeze through. There's only one really narrow bit near the beginning. For a horrible moment I thought I was really stuck. But after that it widens out and it's easy."

"What was it like?" Father asked.

"There's about ten feet of passage and it opens up into this big cave, with stalactites. Nothing spectacular, like Carlsbad, just rather moth-eaten brown ones hanging from ceiling. There was a lot of fallen rock at the far end — there could be a way through there — and I could hear the sound of water quite loudly. I sure hated to come back, Dad. By next year I'm going to be too big to get through." It was a plea, but Father was adamant.

"There is no way I'm going to allow you to go exploring by yourself, Jack. You should never have gone through that crack alone — suppose you had got stuck?"

Jack tried to look abashed, but not very successfully, and Father went on. "If you're right about the cave going on behind the fallen rock there might be another entrance farther round the mountain. It might be worth having a look."

But though we spent the rest of the morning combing the side of the mountain we could find no sign of another way in. There was just a narrow fissure, smaller than my hand, through which a stream of ice-cold water trickled down the mountainside to join the stream from our mountain just above the treeline. Right there, close to the crack, the bittersweet smell of the cave was suddenly in my nostrils again, and I shivered in spite of the sun.

Eventually we gave up and went back to camp for lunch. "What are we going to do this afternoon?" Jack asked with his mouth full of cheese sandwich.

"It'll be a scorcher in another hour." Father looked up at the cloudless sky. "I think Barry and Doug and I will take today's samples and maps down to the shade of the trees and study them down there. What about you two?"

I felt Jack's wish at the same time as he must have felt mine. We spoke together.

"I think Julia'd rather go exploring."

"I'm sure Jack'd rather go with you guys."

Then we both had to laugh at Doug's and Barry's bewildered expressions. "We'll go exploring, Dad," Jack said firmly. "Down in the valley, where it's nice and cool."

"Be back before the sun dips behind the mountain. Remember how fast it gets dark up here." With his pipe clamped between his teeth Father began to collect notebooks, magnifying glass and the rest of the paraphernalia together. Jack and I slipped away down the trail into the forest.

It was wonderfully cool and dark among the pines

and spruces, and we walked along briskly. We both knew where we were going.

"You're still convinced about those lights?"

"I'm more sure than ever that it wasn't a dream. And my watch did stop and start again for no reason."

"Marsh gas, maybe? Or the reflection of car lights from the highway?"

"If you'd been awake you wouldn't have suggested anything so dumb," I retorted. "Look, see for yourself." I grabbed his hand and sent him a picture of the spinning lights, the strange prickly feeling, the great shadow soaring above the tents.

"Wow!" Jack stared at me. "No wonder you were scared. That looked *real*..."

"I'm sure it was. And if the look-out man can back me up..."

"But we won't talk about UFOs. Just say we saw some lights and see how he reacts."

"He'll probably be official-type dumb."

But I was wrong. When we staggered to the top of the zigzag trail and wiped the sweat out of our eyes we were greeted by a university student in cut-offs and sandals, with an impressive tan and an enormous red beard. He greeted us as if we were long-lost friends and parked us in the shade behind his hut with glasses of cold lemonade.

When we'd recovered we told him who we were and asked about safety of the water. He shook hands formally. "I'm Dave Ross. The water's fine. It comes straight out of the side of the mountain and it's as pure as it can get. It's got a funny sort of taste, but the analysis says it's perfectly okay. In fact since I've been drinking it the ulcer I've had all year seems to have cleared up completely."

"Maybe the rest and the fresh air?" Jack suggested.

"Perhaps. But I think it's the water. This post has the reputation of being unusually healthy. You finished with your drinks? Then how about climbing the tower? You go up first and hold on tight. Luckily there's no wind. Sometimes it's like being in a ship at sea."

It was some climb. The rungs were just round metal rods, easy to slip off, and every footstep echoed and jangled from top to bottom of the cagelike structure. I only looked down once. The ground started to spin around below me and I clung on and shut my eyes. You can't get sea-sick on dry land, you nut, I told myself. Then I felt Jack in my mind, steadying me, and I wiped my slippery hands against my jeans and went on climbing.

Once we were in the tower, with the trapdoor shut, it was great. The walls were breast high, so I didn't feel I was going to tip over. I could see the whole range of the Rockies from south to north across the western horizon, while like a dark sea below and around us lay the forest that the fire-tower was here to protect. The whole landscape shimmered in the heat, and I had to squint my eyes against the reflected light off the mountains. I looked across the valley to the scree-covered saddle we had crossed six hours before and searched for the entrance to the cave. From this angle, too, it was completely hidden.

There was a thing like a sun-dial in the middle of the room, marked with a compass rose and with a movable arm. I sighted along the pointer and moved it around till I could see our tents, up on the plateau opposite. Due west, give or take a point.

"How often are you up here?" I asked casually.

"Every hour during the day and a couple of times at night. Of course during electrical storms I'm on duty constantly. We have to log all strikes as possible fire sources. But that's not as bad as it sounds. We've had no storms to speak of this year."

"Many aircraft?"

Not a one. We're way off the commercial fly-paths and you don't find small stuff flying around in the mountains except near communities with landing strips, like Banff."

"That's funny. I saw some lights last night. I thought it was a big jet at first." I looked up at Dave as innocently as I knew how. He stroked his red beard as if it were a pet and looked back at me. He had sparky blue eyes, but for the life of me I couldn't tell what he was thinking. After a minute he seemed to make his mind up about something.

"Let's go on down. I'll make us a pot of tea. Or there's some of the lemonade left, if you'd rather. I'll go first. Close the trap door as you come."

He slid down over the edge with the ease of long practice and I followed, fumbling nervously with my feet. He caught my ankles and guided me firmly to the rungs. It wasn't too bad going down. He was such a big man I felt that if I did slip I'd fall soft. I looked back up when my feet were on firm ground. The lookout seemed immensely far away and tiny, silhouetted against the blue sky. I felt a proud glow at having made it to the top. And I sure was glad I wouldn't have to do it again. Like the cave...never again!

Dave invited us into his hut. It was dark and cool inside and very tidy. There was a small propane stove, a heater and a fridge. There was a bunk against one wall, a large wooden table with stacks of books, and a couple of chairs. In the corner was an impressive-looking radio-telephone.

We sat at the table while he moved around getting tea. He didn't seem to be in any hurry to talk, so we just sat quietly, looking around. Finally he poured tea and handed out cookies.

"So you've seen lights, have you? Where and when?" His manner was casual, but I could feel a prickly tension underneath.

"In the valley. Last night, at two o'clock, due west of here."

"You seem very sure of yourself. Two o'clock — sure you weren't dreaming?"

"She spoke to me at the time," Jack put in quietly.

"Mmm. Marsh-gas?"

"No way. It had a shadow — a big one."

"A shadow? I've never seen that!"

"Then you have seen something?" Jack was on to it like a terrier.

"Yeah. I guess so. Lights. They tend to hover around the lake and the stream. That's what made me think of marsh-gas. It's pretty swampy down by the lake."

"Do you put them in your reports?" Jack asked curiously.

"No way! Just lightning strikes, smokes..."

"Suppose the lights weren't just marsh-gas? Suppose they belonged to something — something with a shadow, something big?"

"You mean like Unidentified Flying Objects? Boy, I'd have to be sure of my facts before I'd put anything like that down in an official report! Look, I've had this summer job for two years now. It's paid for my tuition and most of my books. Good summer jobs are scarcer than hens' teeth these days. No, little green men would have to come marching in this door before I'd report anything like that to headquarters...but those lights sure are weird."

"I suppose there'd be no point in reporting them anyway. What could anyone do about them?"

"Oh, I suppose the ranger station would notify the RCMP. Or the army. Not that you kids have a thing to worry about. There won't be an invasion from outer space just because we've all seen a few lights!"

CHAPTER THREE

We clambered carefully down the hot stony trail. The sun was in the west now, shining full on us as we negotiated boulders and trailing briars. At the bottom of the hill I stopped.

"Let's take some pop up to the camp. And maybe the rest of the hamburger, if it's defrosted."

"Bound to be, in this heat."

"I don't know. It was frozen hard and it's a good cooler."

We found the station wagon parked in the brush and loaded up with three pounds of hamburger and all the pop we could carry.

"I'll make spaghetti and meatballs tonight, and then tomorrow we'll have to start on the cans and freeze-dried stuff."

As we walked slowly through the dark wood I could hear water over on our left. "Let's walk up the stream, Jacko. I'm still thirsty, but I don't feel like pop."

The trees grew close, with jagged branches ready to catch and tear, and we had to be careful. It was worth it, though. The stream had mossy banks covered with tiny pale flowers. It was cool there. I knelt down to drink and to splash my hot face. It was wonderfully icy.

"Jack, the water does have the oddest taste. Not a bit like the stream up by our camp."

He drank too, cautiously at first and then deeply. "Oh, that is good."

"It reminds me of something and I can't think what."

"Me too. Not long ago...today. I remember, Julia. It was in the cave."

"The strange smell in the cave is like the taste of this water...bittersweet. How weird."

"Maybe not so weird, Jule. Remember the stream that came out of the mountain not far from the cave? Well, if there were something inside the cave to give the water that strange taste it might also account for the smell. I'm sure that stream, *this* stream, is the running water I heard."

"I wonder what it is. It's strange."

"I can guess. I never told you everything I saw in

the inner cave. You were still hating it and I didn't want to make it worse by going on.''

"Well, it's okay here in the open. Tell me...no, better still, show me.''

I could see the crease between his dark eyebrows as he concentrated. This was something special we could do, but it was hard work, not like our everyday mind-talking. He reached out for my hand and at once I was right inside his mind, looking through his eyes.

Jack...I...was back in the cave, pushing and wriggling along the narrow passage. Then the space opened up and I could see the flashlight dancing on the ceiling, where the stalactites hung like dirty rock candy. The sound of running water was close by. And water shone on the left hand wall of the cave. In the flashlight's beam I could see, growing around the seepage, a curious fungus. It was a pallid greyish-white and close to it the strange bitter-sweet smell was very strong.

I blinked and suddenly was back in the cool wood by the little stream, with Jack's hand in mine. The same smell lingered faintly in the air, like a memory.

"That was fun, being you, enjoying the cave instead of having claustrophobia. So the fungus causes the odd smell and taste. I'm glad Dave told us the water was extra healthy. I'd have expected it to be poisonous, dripping over that horrid-looking stuff.''

"So that's one mystery cleared up. But about the lights..."

"Jack, should I tell Father and the guys?"

"I think you should. They might see something themselves."

"I bet they laugh at me, Barry anyway," I said gloomily.

I was right. When I told them what I'd seen, after supper, Barry just rolled around laughing. Jack tried to stand up for me and Barry challenged him.

"Did you honestly see something yourself? One girl's testimony isn't worth much."

I could have hit him. Jack said carefully, "I saw exactly what Julia's described to you." He didn't say he'd only seen it in my mind. Barry didn't believe him anyway. I could tell.

"Well, it's not important." I shrugged. "But I thought it was kind of interesting, especially when Dave Ross said he'd seen lights too. Time for bed, anyway."

I was wakened with a sense of deep excitement and sat up in bed. Had I been dreaming? I leaned on one elbow and peered at my watch. Just before midnight. I'd been asleep for nearly three hours. I could hear Father's steady breathing a few feet away from my head. I relaxed, ready for sleep again, and then suddenly realised that it was Jack's excitement I could feel.

He had seen something so incredible that his emotion had bridged the distance between us and wakened me.

I crept towards the door of the tent, unzipped the screen and stood up outside. The sky was very black, and a full moon flooded the valley and the mountain slopes with a bluish-white light that made a mockery out of depth and distance. It looked unreal, like the set for a space movie.

Nobody moved in the other tent. It was all very quiet. I walked towards the slope above the forest. The grass was cool and damp under my bare feet and a chill breeze ruffled my cotton pyjamas.

I reached the edge of the plateau just in time. Slowly, noiselessly, the disc was settling among the trees near the stream. The pines were about eight feet apart down there, and as the silver-grey disc sank to the ground I heard on the quiet night air a great crack, and three of the trees trembled, splayed out and fell. There were no lights. No other sound. Just a round grey *thing*, settling on the forest floor like a moth, pushing trees out of its way as if they were matches.

I remembered the splintered tree that Jack and I had dragged up to the camp, the other tree, still standing, with its tip snapped off, and the joke about flying elephants. Whatever this thing was, it had landed here before.

Where on earth was Jack? I whispered his name and caught an inward response from way down the trail. I whirled to the left and caught a glimpse of white T-shirt as he dodged from tree to tree on the trail far below me. I forgot caution and screamed out loud. "Jack! Jack, come back!"

The only response was an inward laugh, a catch-me-if-you-can feeling. Jack always loved danger, and I was always afraid. This time he was heading for something too powerful, too alien, and somehow I had to stop him.

I dashed into the tent for my shoes and jacket. Father was sitting up, still cocooned in sleeping bag, his hair rumpled and sticking up on top. Without his glasses he looked like an oversized boy.

"There's a UFO. Down in the valley. It's real," I gasped, fighting with the knots in the laces of my runners. "Jack's gone after it by himself, and I've got to stop him."

As I ran from the tent I could hear Father's voice calling me, but I ran on, straight over the edge and down the steep slope into the forest. I hadn't thought of bringing a flashlight, but the moon seemed to make everything as clear as day. That turned out to be deceptive. I found myself avoiding black bars that were only shadows and then tripping over roots and brambles that lay silvery invisible in the flat moonlight. I was bruised and scratched and breathless, but I plunged on down the slope, trying to reach the strange silver disc before Jack.

It was much darker down among the densely growing trees of the valley floor. The moonlight made only faint pools of light in the occasional clearing. I pushed on.

At first I thought the glow was another patch of moonlight; but it was greener, more luminous. It glimmered almost straight ahead. I darted from tree to tree, as fast as I dared, walking on the soft moss, trying not to snap twigs. My mind reached out to Jack, begging him to stop, to come back. A silent laugh answered me, over to my left. I turned and saw Jack's T-shirt white in the moonlight.

"Stay where you are, Jule. These skinny pines won't hide two of us. I'll be careful. But I simply have to see."

The words came into my mind as clearly as if Jack were whispering in my ear. I acknowledged them, but crept forward from tree to tree, ever closer to the luminous glow.

My heart was pounding right up in my throat and it was hard to breathe steadily. I was no more than ten yards away, Jack a little closer. As we crouched in the shelter of neighbouring trees the greenish light began to strengthen and the prickly feeling crawled over my skin again. I could feel the hairs on the back of my arms stir as if I was suddenly cold. Then the light faded and went out altogether. Cautiously we peered out from behind our trees.

The UFO was lying in a clearing of its own making. I could see the gleam of fresh wood where the pines had snapped and splintered under the force of the thing. It gleamed grey, metallic, in the moonlight. It was about twelve feet across, I suppose, curving up to eight feet at the domed centre, with a thick doughnut-like ring around the perimeter. There seemed to be no doors, no windows. At the dome's top something flashed. I could *feel* Jack's intense curiosity.

"Don't, Jacko!" I called out. But it was no good. He crept forward slowly towards the shelter of a large pine that almost touched the outer rim of the UFO. He was as silent as a shadow, but as he moved a light shot down from the dome, catching hm squarely in its narrow greenish beam.

I shrank back against my tree, feeling the coarse bark against my face. Jack stood perfectly still, frozen in the light beam. One foot was off the ground and one hand out in front of his face. I reached out desperately into his mind.

"Jacko! Jacko, run!"

There was no response, nothing at all. I was reaching out to an emptiness as complete as if my brother did not exist.

The light modulated. There was a faint low-pitched hum. Jack lowered his hand and put his foot down. He raised the other foot...slowly. Put it down. Walked...step...by...step...towards...the...UFO. Where a moment before the surface had been smoothly silver a narrow oblong of shadow appeared. An open door.

I ran out from behind my tree, screaming. I didn't care what happened to me. I was so close to Jack that I could reach out my hand and...

Two cruelly hard hands caught me from behind and lifted me off the ground. Hurled me to one side. I heard rather than felt the crash of broken branches as I landed, and then I blacked out.

CHAPTER FOUR

I felt soft moss under my back. There were low voices and the rippling sound and bitter-sweet smell of the stream close by. I moved and groaned. Every muscle ached, and beyond the ache was something far worse, something I couldn't quite remember. A hand came over my mouth, gentle but firm.

"Hush, Julia. It's all right. Don't make a noise." It was Doug's voice. I opened my eyes and tried to sit up. My head spun and I slumped back again. I was lying on the mossy bank of the stream. I could see moonlight dancing on the ripples. I rolled over and splashed my face and then drank from my cupped hand. It tasted good and my head began to clear. Soon I would be able to remember whatever it was.

I managed to sit up and looked wonderingly at the

boys. Doug's dark face was inscrutable, but even in the flicker of moonlight and shadow I could see how white Barry was, how his hands trembled and how a nerve beside his mouth twitched. Why were they looking at me in that...that *compassionate* way?

. And suddenly I remembered. "Jack! They got Jack!"

Doug's hand was over mine, warm, steadying. "Yes, Julia, I'm afraid they did."

"Where's Father? I've got to tell Father." I looked wildly round.

"Julia, they got him too." His arms went round me as I tried to jump to my feet.

"Oh, no, no!"

'Shut up!" Barry's voice was panicky. "They'll get us *all* if you make all that noise."

"Be quiet, Barry. Listen, Julia. Do you remember you were going after Jack? Well, Mr. Christie caught up with you and pulled you out of the way. Then he tried to save Jack, but the beam trapped him. It was like a magnet. It drew them both into the UFO and the door shut again. Nothing's happened since."

I found myself sobbing wildly, my face buried in Doug's jacket. I stopped suddenly and put my hand over my mouth. I mustn't make a noise. Barry was right. But Father and Jack both...

"Listen, Julia. They haven't taken off. If they

wanted to capture people for...something, surely they'd take off right away. But they haven't. Don't give up hope."

I wiped my hand over my wet face and sniffed hard. "Doug, what are we going to do?"

Barry stood up. "I'll tell you," he whispered. His voice trembled. "We're going to tell the RCMP, the army, whatever it takes to get this thing destroyed before it gets the rest of us. I'm going to the lookout tower."

"Barry, no! Father and Jack are inside. We can't do anything that might hurt them. Oh, Barry, stop!"

Barry had begun to run downstream towards Lookout Mountain. In a few seconds he was out of sight among the shadows, but we could hear the crashing of branches as he blundered through the dark forest.

"Oh, Doug, please stop him. At least till we've had a chance to think. If he tells the police or the army they'll just blow up the UFO, or scare it off. They won't care about Father and Jack. Please, Doug."

"Stay here. I'll stop him." He was off, his feet noiseless on the moss and pine needles, dodging as swiftly among the trees as if it were broad daylight.

I could no longer hear Barry. The forest was silent and very dark. The moon was setting behind out mountain. In a couple of hours it would be dawn. A chilly breeze ran down the slope, and I shivered and backed up against a tree trunk and sat there hugging my knees for warmth.

There was nothing to see, and yet I felt a hundred eyes peering at me from behind every tree. Suppose the aliens were prowling through the forest right this minute, looking for me? What would they be like, I wondered with a shudder. Would they by many-legged horrors like intelligent tarantulas? Or lumps of amoeba-like jelly? Or perhaps, worst of all, pure intelligences with no bodies at all that I could fight back against to get at Father and Jack.

A twig snapped behind me and my hand went up to my mouth. I wanted to shout after Doug to come back, not to leave me alone. If I could only contact Jack. I tried again and again, but there was no telepathic link between us at all. It was like last summer when he was down at Cypress Hills. I hadn't been able to reach Jack then. Now he was only a few minutes away, but we were cut off completely.

What could be happening to Jack and Father while I was sitting here, feeling sorry for myself? I looked around. There was no sign of the UFO, and I had no idea how far Doug and Barry had carried me. There was no green glimmer, only dark trees against a darker background. I tried to reason it out. In a panic, dragging an unconscious girl, surely they would have automatically gone downhill, the easy way, towards the stream.

I stood up unsteadily, gathering the shreds of my resolution around me. Anything was better than sitting waiting for them to creep up on me, I told myself. I turned my back on the stream and began to walk slowly forward into the dark forest, bearing to my left, uphill.

I must have crept along, feeling my way, for about five minutes. I don't know. Time and space seemed stretched out to monstrous lengths that night. But finally I saw it between the trees, almost dead ahead, sitting in its clearing, surrounded by splintered pines. It glowed faintly with a pearly greenish light. There was no sign of life. There was no open door. It was smooth all the way around. It didn't look as if there could ever have been a door.

I don't know what I had expected to happen, or what I had planned to do. I just know that I felt suddenly completely empty and tired, unbelievably tired. I sank down on the ground behind the safety of a tree and closed my eyes. I called out to Jack in my mind with what strength I had left. I called again and again, to be answered only by loneliness, emptiness.

It must have been a change in the faint vibration

from the UFO that made me open my eyes and look up. I saw the light fade as it had faded when we first came upon it. And the same instant Jack was in my mind again.

"Jule, where've you been? I've been trying to get you for hours!" His fear and loneliness somehow gave me the strength I needed.

"I couldn't reach you. Are you all right? And Dad? What's happening?"

"I don't know. We're not hurt, but we can't move, either of us. Oh, Jule, I'm scared." His fear washed over me in a wave of gooseflesh. I'd helped Jack out of plenty of scrapes of his own making, but never had he been afraid of anything before. The surprise steadied me.

"Take your time, Jacko. I'm right outside this UFO thing and I can hear you as clearly as could be. But don't let them put that light on again. I think that's what interfered before."

There was a pause. Then Jack's voice came clearly in my mind. "I think they know that. That's why they turned it off. But it's some kind of protection. They'll have to turn it on again if anyone else comes close."

"How do you know *that*?"

"That's funny. I suppose they must have put the idea in my head."

"Do you think they just want to be friendly? To...talk?"

"Maybe. I wish you were here too. No, I don't. It'd be awful for you. I'm glad you got away. I'm sorry, Jule. It was all my fault."

"Forget it, Jacko. Tell me what it's like inside that thing. Maybe it'll give me an idea of what to do." At least it'll take your mind off things, I thought, and I caught a faint chuckle in my mind as he realised what I was doing. We never could keep secrets from each other.

"It's, oh, dim and yet shiny at the same time. There's a lot of funny looking stuff, not machinery, but I suppose that's what it is. Oh, I just wish you could *see* ..."

As he spoke my mind filled with swirling greens like the Northern Lights, and then suddenly I was there, inside the UFO, in a small domed room that shone softly like the inside of an oyster shell. I was inside Jack's mind and his body too, sitting on a bench which curved around the perimeter of the room. The floor was covered with the same soft resilient stuff as the bench and it was faintly luminous.

As I tried to look around I realised that Jack was a prisoner in his own body. He could breathe, swallow, blink and move his eyes. But that was all. He couldn't so much as wiggle a toe. I moved my eyes to the right. I could just see Father, a prisoner too. I wished I could get inside his mind, talk to him too.

Across the room was a huge console covered with dials and buttons. In the very centre of the dome a thick pillar rose from floor to ceiling. It glowed greenish. It was very quiet and dim.

I didn't see the figures at first. Perhaps they didn't want me too. These were really and truly aliens, creatures from another planet, another solar system, perhaps even another galaxy, though vaguely I remembered that that was impossible. They were very tall, the figures standing by the console, and they looked almost human. It was just that they were so *very* tall, and their legs seemed a little too short, their arms too long and spindly to be human.

They were clothed from head to toe in silvery coveralls with hoods, and their faces were shadowed by transparent visors. As I watched, through Jack's eyes, one of the three came towards us. He came so close that I could see his face, shadowed, greenish, his eyes large and pale with a slit pupil like a cat's. As he stooped over us I could feel Jack's panic surging over both of us. The alien's mind reached out to us. I gasped and let go.

I opened my eyes to the chilly forest. I felt numb and unreal, as if I was still in the middle of a nightmare. Was that real, that squat shape among the familiar trees? Had I truly seen aliens, face to face? How long had I been sitting here? Had Doug stopped Barry from reaching the lookout?

I got stiffly to my feet. Dawn had lightened the sky to a pale blue-green and the stars had gone, except for Venus, shining low in the east to the right of Lookout Mountain. The UFO began to glow again. Was someone coming? I listened and after a while heard a stick crack. It must be the boys. I went back to the stream to wait for them. I longed to see real people again, to hear real voices.

We met by the stream. Even in the half-light I could see that Barry had a swollen lip and eye and that the collar of his pyjama jacket was torn. Doug looked as calm and unruffled as ever.

Oh, the relief! I began to tell them what I'd seen, but the words wouldn't come out right and I began to shake and sob. Doug seemed to understand. He took my arm. "We can't talk here. We'll go up to the camp, make a good fire and have breakfast. Then you can tell us what happened and we'll decide what to do."

I nodded gratefully and let him help me through the trees and up the steep path to the camp, with Barry sulking along behind.

The camp looked unbelievably normal, the tents, the

fireplace, the kettle and the coffee pot, just where we had left them. It was like coming to a totally different world, the normal world. While Doug made the fire I went into our tent. Father's sleeping bag lay in a heap in the middle of the floor. Mechanically I picked it up and shook it out. There was a faint whiff of the tobacco he used. My eyes suddenly stung. Oh, Daddy, will I ever see you again?

But I wasn't a baby any more and there was work to do, even if I didn't understand yet what it was to be. I skinned out of my pyjamas and into jeans, shirt and sweater. The neat piles of provisions by the tent door reminded me that I was supposed to be cook. I grabbed a loaf of bread, a can of bacon and the coffee.

"Good girl!" Doug's smile warmed me. He spooned the coffee into the pot boiling on the fire. A dash of cold water to settle the ground and it was ready, the best camp coffee I ever had. I sat as close to the fire as I could get with my mug in my hands. The fire crackled cheerfully, and the sun, just cutting the eastern horizon, seemed to tell me that it was all just a nightmare and nightmares do not survive the light of day.

I had two cups of hot sweet coffee, but shook my head when Doug offered me a bacon sandwich. "I couldn't eat a thing, honestly."

"Come on, Julia. Try a little. We don't know

what we may have to do today. You've been up all night. Fainting from hunger won't help your father or Jack.''

So I chewed on a sandwich and washed down the hard lump of it with more coffee. But I did begin to feel warmer.

"Okay, Julia? Do you think you can talk now?''

"Sure, I'm fine. I'm sorry I was so shook up before. Look, it's terribly important that we don't tell the RCMP or anyone else who might scare off the aliens, not till we find out what they want. Father and Jack are prisoners all right, but they're perfectly safe so far. I think the aliens want to talk to them.''

"She's flipped out! She's completely flipped!''

"Julia, what are you talking about? How can you possibly know...?''

"Oh!'' I looked at their shocked faces and wished that Jack and I hadn't been quite so secretive about our telepathy. How could I make the boys believe me now, when it mattered? "Look, you guys, you know Jack and I are twins. Well, we have this special kind of thing together...''

"Yeah, yeah. You've got this feeling he's okay.'' Barry was scornful.

"No, it's not that. It's much more. We can read each other's mind. We always have. Usually just feelings and ideas, sometimes actual words as if we were talking, only nobody else can hear. But if we work at it really hard we can see things through each other's eyes, just as if we were the other person. Do you see?''

"Telepathy? That's just a lot of malarkey. It's not scientific.''

"Maybe you can't measure it, Barry, but it happens.'' Doug interrupted. "Our wise men used to be trained to do just that. Myself, I met an old shaman once who could step inside minds. He used his gift to heal people who had bad spirits.''

"Yes, Doug, that's it. Oh, Barry, please believe me and at least *try* to understand. Look, do you remember when I ran out of the cave yesterday? I had got inside Jack's mind by accident just as he was wriggling through that crack into the inner cave. I could feel everything he was feeling, the weight of the mountain, the feeling of being trapped. It scared me so much I had to get out.''

"I wondered what you were fussing about. But what has that to do with it?''

"When Doug went after you I sat down close to the UFO, and I found I could get in touch with Jack once more. I saw inside that thing, the aliens, Jack, Father, everything.'' I told them exactly what it had been like. Even Barry was impressed. He sat with his cup dangling, his mouth open. "...So you see it's absolutely vital that we don't scare them off while they've still got Father and Jack. And if they have that force-field on I can't reach Jack."

"Okay, I agree. Doug, I'm sorry about what happened."

Doug grinned. "Forget it. It was a good fight. My ribs still ache."

"Really?" Barry's voice brightened and he managed a smile past his split lip. I could see that his left eye was swelling up beautifully.

"Julia, are you in touch with Jack now?"

"No. They switched on the force-field when you came through the trees."

"Would you let me use Mr. Christie's binoculars?" Doug asked, and when I brought them he looked down into the wooded valley. When you knew what you were looking for you could see the splintered tops of pines where the UFO had landed, but nothing else. The sun was shining straight in our eyes and casting long shadows down among the trees. There was no sign of movement.

"I don't think he'll see anything from the lookout," Doug said finally. He scanned the mountain and the firetower. "He must still be asleep. Nothing's moving over there."

"I've got to go down to the UFO again." It was hard to say the words. It made it real again.

"Julia, you're crazy!"

"You don't understand, Barry. I have to be there in case Jack wants to get in touch with me. Maybe the aliens will let them go. Maybe they want something. I don't know what it's all about, but I know I've got to be there."

"But it's too dangerous. They might suck you in with that beam."

"They didn't when I was there before." I looked down at the dark forest and shivered. "But you don't have to come. I can go by myself." Even to my ears the words sounded hollow.

"Of course we'll come with you, Julia. What do you think we are? Right, Barry?"

"I guess so. But we should find out what we're up against. We don't know what that force-field is, or the green ray. They could be radioactive. I think we should take the geiger counter and test the area first. I wish Mr. Christie had a gun"

"A gun? Oh, Barry! You still don't understand. I really don't think they want to hurt us. I have to go anyway, radiation or no radiation. Jack and Father are there."

"We'll take the geiger counter anyway and some provisions and the compass."

Okay, then.'' Doug threw the coffee dregs into the fire and carefully sprinkled dirt over the remaining embers.

By seven o'clock we were making our way down the stream bed into the forest. The coffee had made me feel warm and alert, and now it was broad daylight I was finding it hard to go on believing that Father and Jack had been kidnapped by aliens. I couldn't really believe in aliens. Jays and woodpeckers were screaming cheerfully to each other. Above our heads a squirrel scolded as we passed his territory. The stream shuckled over the stones.

I suppose it was the noise of the birds and the water that prevented him from hearing us until we were almost on top of him. He was bending over the stream, filling some sort of container. The sun gleamed silver on his coverall.

Barry was in front. He stopped dead and drew in a breath so loud it was a groan. In a flash Doug's hand was over his mouth, but it was too late. The alien looked up, saw us and turned to face us before we could move. The water container was in one hand, but the other pointed at us what could only be, in spite of its unfamiliar shape, a weapon.

CHAPTER FIVE

We froze. I mean literally froze. I felt a strange tingling sensation, like the feeling you get when there's a bad electric storm coming, and when it was over it was as if my arms and legs were encased in warm marble. I could move my eyes enough to see Doug and Barry just ahead and slightly to the right of me, but that was all I could move. Doug's hand was frozen over Barry's mouth. Barry's arms were out in front of him as if pushing away a nightmare.

The alien came closer and looked us over. Can there be anything so impenetrable as a space visor? I couldn't even begin to imagine what he was thinking, or what he planned to do now we were in his power. What actually happened was a anticlimax to my horrifying thoughts. The alien calmly turned his back on us and walked away through the trees towards the UFO, leaving us standing by the stream, frozen.

In the distance I heard a faint but distinct hum, like an angry bee. Quite suddenly I could feel again. I had pins and needles all over. It was agony. I gasped and found I could move. I hobbled over to a tree and leaned against it while I rubbed my arms and legs and flexed my toes and fingers. The others were hopping around too, as the freezing wore off them.

"No we *know* what they're capable of, Julia." Barry was shivering. "We've got to warn the police or the army. Next time they could *kill* us."

"But they've just shown us that they don't need to do that." Doug reasoned. "I don't think they mean to do us any harm at all."

"Doug's right, Barry. That alien could just as easily have zapped us, but he didn't. All he did was stop us from doing anything stupid while he got away to safety. There's a good reason for everything they're doing, there has to be. If we call in the police we'll never find out what the aliens want, or get Father or Jack back."

"And if they kill us or kidnap us we'll never get them back or find out what they're after, and then it'll be too late to wish we'd gone for help. No, count me out!"

"Barry, You're not going to quit on us? We have to help Julia get Mr. Christie and Jack back."

"The only way is to go for help. It's the only thing that makes sense."

Just then, as we stood under the trees by the sunny stream, arguing furiously at the tops of our voices, I heard something, something meant for me.

"Oh, shush, you guys, and listen."

It came again, a hollow sound like a voice from deep inside a cave.

"Come!"

"I don't hear anything, Julia. What was it?"

"Me neither. Stop wasting time. We've got to go for help."

"Come!"

"It's calling me. I've got to go."

"No, Julia. There's nothing there. Don't you see, it's a trap. They'll get *you* next. Then Doug. And me."

Take it easy, Barry. It's okay, Julia. We'll come with you."

"Not me." Barry twisted his arm out of Doug's grip and was off, dodging among the trees, downstream towards Lookout Mountain.

"Come!"

It was like a drumbeat, tuned to the rhythm of my heart. I was cold and shivery, but I knew I had to go. I was grateful when Doug grabbed my hand. His was warm, and his face was as calm as if unheard voices called one into the forest every day of the week. Together we followed the path the alien had taken. After a few steps the stream was hidden and in a few more the silvery gleam of the UFO showed among the shadowy trees ahead of us.

"Wait, Julia," Doug whispered. He slipped the haversack off his shoulder.

I didn't want to wait. I wanted to hurry. Somebody needed me. "Oh, Doug, what *is* it?"

He dug in the haversack and pulled out the compass, which was on top. "Hang on to this for a moment, while I get out the geiger counter. I think Barry was right about one thing. We should check for radiation. Maybe it isn't safe to stay so close."

The geiger counter was big and cornery and right at the bottom. I shivered with impatience as Doug got it out. He dumped the haversack against a tree and walked slowly forward, watching the indicator of the counter. The UFO glowed softly like a great greenish pearl. The needle on the indicator didn't budge.

"I guess it's safe enough." Doug put it down and held out his hand for the compass.

"Doug, look!" The compass in my hand had gone mad. The hand pointed east, then west, swithered and spun round and round.

Doug's dark eyes gleamed. "Magnetic force,

not nuclear! I'll bet your watch has stopped again."

I gave him the useless compass and looked at my watch. Seven twenty-five. That should be about the right time. Then I noticed that the second hand had stopped. I got the spooky idea that the aliens had frozen time. I shivered.

"My watch has stopped too. Don't be scared, Julia. There must be an intense magnetic field around that thing, but it won't hurt us. What happens now?"

"I don't know." The drumbeat command had stopped, and I stood wondering what on earth I was doing. But I felt tired, terribly tired. My knees gave and I sank down against a pine tree. "Just ...got to...wait." I yawned and in spite of everything that had happened my eyelids drooped shut.

Instantly I felt that I was back inside the UFO. Part of me was within Jack, feeling his feelings, sharing his thoughts; but this time part of me seemed to be hovering in the air above him, watching what was going on.

Two of the aliens were sitting on the bench, one on either side of Jack, and one held a silver-gloved hand to Jack's forehead. I could see Jack's face with the freckles standing out like crayon dots and a rim of white around his eye like a startled horse.

The air was a mishmash of signals. I was getting bits of alien ideas, bits of Father's anxiety, but from Jack nothing but a jangling panic. It was like trying to translate at an angry UN assembly. The static was drowning out the sense.

I took a deep breath and got in as close as I could to Jack's mind. It was closer than I had ever managed before. It was as if we were two personalities in one skin. "Hey, brother! Quit yelling and listen!"

He stopped struggling right away and a little colour came back to his face. "Oh, Jule, thank goodness you're back. I thought you'd gone for good."

"As if I would, Jacko. I came back as soon as I could. Now listen. Our telepathy's fantastically strong, do you notice? I think the aliens have souped up the signal in some way. Which means they need us — you and me — to get some kind of message across. I don't think they mean to hurt us. Don't be scared. If you can just relax and let them go ahead, maybe they'll be satisfied and let you go."

"That's all very well to say, Jule, but you don't know what it's like. This fellow, the one with his hand on my head, I think he's trying to hypnotize me. It's horrible!"

"I do know, Jacko, truly. I can feel it too. But you've simply got to trust them. Relax and let them in. Don't fight it. There isn't any other way."

"Yeah, I know. Only...well, okay. Wish me luck, Jule. Here I go."

He closed his eyes and relaxed. He went limp so suddenly it scared even me who knew what was happening, and Father thought he'd fainted and tried desperately to help him. The alien next to Father pushed him gently back onto the bench and refroze him with the thing we'd thought was a weapon.

Poor Father! He didn't know what was going on at all. He didn't even suspect that I was right inside the UFO watching him. I wished I could have got into his mind and reassured him, but I couldn't. The telepathy only worked between Jack and me.

The domed room glowed in pale iridescent colours that shimmered and changed as I waited. I tried to empty my mind of all its fears. Just to accept. It was very quiet. From the pillar in the centre of the room came an almost inaudible hum. The third alien moved silently, monitoring instruments at the huge console.

Then the aliens began to speak to me through Jack. There were no words, of course. Even among themselves they did not always use words. They sent me pictures, ideas. Sometimes a concept made no sense at all and I'd send a question back. Patiently the aliens would send me a new idea and then another, until I got it clearly, and then we would go on. Finally I understood their story down to the last detail.

Something else came across to me very clearly beside

their story and that was their character. I had the strong sense of a sad and noble race making a last desperate effort to save their species from extinction. I was no longer afraid of them. I wanted to be friends. I was sorry that we couldn't breathe the same air, share the same food, that we must be for ever separated by the silver fabric and face visors that served to protect them from the bacteria and viruses of our planet.

I wanted to help for their sake now, as well as for Jack and Father. I sent this message to them with all the warmth I was capable of. Then I looked for the last time around the shell-like room, at Father and Jack sitting side by side on the padded bench, the tall silvery aliens beside them. I didn't want to leave just yet, but I knew I had to go. There was work to be done and there was very little time left. Slowly I let go my link with Jack. The lights faded.

I was outside the UFO again, sitting against a pine, cold and cramped and stiff.

"Julia, are you there? Are you all right?" Doug was holding my arms.

"Yeah." My voice croaked. "Thirsty though. How long was I gone?"

"From the sun I'd say it's nearly noon. Hours anyway. What happened?"

"It's a long story. I'm thirsty and freezing. Let's get

out into the sun and I'll tell you the whole thing."

As we scrambled to out feet, Doug steadying me with a firm hand, a narrow beam of light shot straight as a ruler from the top of the UFO to a spot on the grass directly in front of us. There was a momentary hum, so high-pitched as to be almost unbearable. It stopped and the light was gone. In its place lay a small pearl-white box. As I bent to pick it up Doug grabbed me back.

"Be careful!"

"It's all right, Doug. It's only a container...an empty container." I slipped it into my shirt pocket and then let Doug help me over the broken pine branches and mossy tussocks to the stream.

I drank and drank. The strange water revived me like magic. "Where's Barry?" My mind was beginning to function again.

"I don't know. The second time he ran off I didn't want to leave you alone. You were in some kind of a trance. So I let him go."

"Do you think he really would go for the police?"

Doug shrugged. "I don't know. But even if he did talk to Dave Ross the odds are that Dave wouldn't believe him. You told us he was the sort of person who wouldn't want to make waves."

"I hope I was right. Oh, Doug, I'm so cold. Let's

get out into the sun. We have to climb the mountain anyway.'' I shivered at the thought.

Doug picked up the haversack and walked upstream towards the sunlit meadow below the mountain slope. I followed, feeling the life come back to my legs as I moved. Once we were out of the trees the noonday sun smote down at us. It was wonderful, like a sauna after a long day on the ski-slopes. I could feel it working into my muscles, warming my shoulders and arms and legs. The only thing it couldn't touch was the icy knot in the pit of my stomach.

We went on climbing. The stream splashed fast down the mountainside as the slope grew steeper, until finally it vanished into the cleft in the rock. Here there was a patch of shade and a place where grass and minute alpine flowers grew.

''Let's stop here, Doug, and I'll tell you the aliens' story.''

Unquestioningly he swung the haversack to the ground and dropped down beside it. He took out a couple of candy bars and offered me one, but I shook my head. ''No, thanks, Doug. I'm not hungry.'' I bent and drank from the stream, though. It seemed as if I couldn't get enough of that water.

''I hope it's safe for you to drink that much. We don't really know what's in it.''

I laughed a bit hysterically. "Oh, Doug, you don't know just how safe it really is!"

Then, sitting out on the bare mountainside, looking down into the dark forest which hid Father and Jack and the three aliens, I told Doug the story I had learned when I was inside the UFO.

CHAPTER SIX

The aliens were really not alien at all. Like us they had evolved on Earth, but much earlier, way back at the time when the pressures of increasing drought were forcing ape-man to leave the security of trees and stand on his own two feet and learn to hunt for meat on the grasslands of Africa.

That much was clear. Where they came from I was less certain. Their own name for their native country, *Brini*, had no meaning for me, of course. They sent me pictures of upland meadows greened by flowing streams and dark ancient forests filled with wild life, all enclosed about by huge mountains, the wind forever smoking the snow off their razor-sharp summits. It could have been anywhere in Northern China, India or Tibet. Even Canada or the Andes, I suppose.

They developed air-flight and eventually space flight. I got pictures of their industrial complexes and their machinery, but I couldn't understand it at all. It's as if they had started from a different premise and travelled in a totally different direction than the one we had taken. They didn't use fossil fuels, I'm sure of that, and I don't think they had discovered — or at least chosen to use — atomic power.

Suddenly there came a succession of winters of increasing length. The snow smoking off the mountains obscured the sun for weeks at a time. The streams that irrigated the fields became sealed in ice and every year the glaciers crept a little further down the mountains. The Brinians were surrounded on every side by these mountains. The only thing they could do was to leave by air and start all over again somewhere else.

It was a stupendous undertaking, but it had happened once before, a thousand lifetimes earlier, and that is what they had done then. As before they sent small scouting expeditions to other parts of Earth to find suitable places to resettle, where they could not be threatened by encroaching ice. But this time when the scouts returned they reported the presence of a new species on the face of the earth, a creature balanced on the edge of intelligence.

This changed the whole picture. Had they the right to interfere with this new creature's natural evolution? The Brinians held a council and decided unanimously that rather than disturb the progress of this new man, clumsily shaping tools and weapons, wrapping himself against the cold in the skins of animals, painting his fears and feelings, his needs and memories, on the walls of his cave-home: rather than spoil all this the Brinians voted to leave Earth forever and start afresh on a new planet.

They had very little time. They built a fleet of giant ships. They stored the seeds and grains of Earth, they took every person, grandparents, parents and children, and they left the beautiful land of Brini to be crushed and pounded into powder by the inevitable ice.

They sent me pictures of the immensity of space, of the overwhelming distances between stars, of the lonely void filled only with stellar dust and wisps of gas.

Eventually they found a star with an Earth-like planet, which they decided to make their home. They named it *Brini-la*, which means 'the second Brini'.

The planted their Earth seeds and grains and they grew and flourished. They built new cities after the pattern of the cities of Earth-Brini. There were no great mountains here as there had been on Earth, so they spread out over the whole planet. But they still kept their tradition of government by general assent, and since they had grown in population and were living so far apart they developed telepathy, so that, linked together, they could keep informed and govern Brini-la justly and wisely.

Hundreds of thousands of years passed. Back on Earth the last ice-age had just ended. Man was spreading rapidly down through the Americas. But on Brini-la things were not going so well. Slowly, so slowly that at first they were unaware of it, the momentum was running down. The people were getting tired. There was still no disease, but the life-span of the people was shortening. From two hundred years it dropped to a hundred and ninety-five. Then to a hundred and ninety. The older ones were becoming weakened.

Their whole effort was put into solving the problem, and eventually their scientists came to the conclusion that some trace-mineral or chemical compound that they had brought with them from Earth, in the plants, or even in the bodies of the first settlers, had somehow been used up. And it did not exist on Brini-la. To survive they must isolate it and replenish the supply. They started the long voyage back to Earth, one huge ship, with scientists and doctors.

They crossed the great ocean of space and moored their ship in orbit out beyond the Moon. Here they set up their laboratories, while small craft shuttled to and fro, collecting samples of earth, air, water, plant and animal life.

They observed Man, flourishing in the milder climate that followed the ice-age, banding together in communities, harvesting the wild wheat. They were glad that they had chosen to give him the dignity of growing up by himself.

Before they left on the long trek back to Brini-la they dropped a gift in the fertile soil near the oasis we know today as Jericho. It was the grain of bread wheat, which the Brinians had developed all those years before on Earth and nurtured and husbanded in the two hundred millinia since. They dropped it in the ground and then they went home, to test the samples that seemed to show promise on the fast-aging people of Brini-la.

There was failure after failure and only one small ray of hope. Water from streams in certain mountainous regions of Earth seemed to hold the clue. When the old people drank the water they began to feel better. But whatever the miracle stuff was, it was in amounts too small to analyze.

By now the weakness was spreading. The children were still mercifully free of it, but as more of the older people became affected the whole complex industrial machine began to run down. Soon they would not even have the skill or energy to go back to Earth.

They sent one more ship, smaller and less well equipped, to make the second and perhaps the last journey back to Earth. There were only a few scientific teams this time, one to each continent.

To North America were assigned three young scientists, Kenli, Porri and Jouro. They had only just graduated from university when they were picked to make the trip and now, after nearly ten years of fruitless searching, they were becoming very weary.

Then one summer day, as they were sharing their evening meal in the cramped exploration vehicle that they had come to call 'home,' everything changed. It was a warm evening, almost as pleasant as the evenings on Brini-la; and, hidden among the dark trees, far from any human habitation, they had let their defenses down and left the door open. The warning buzzer brought all three to their feet.

"I don't believe it!"

"It must be another team, Porri."

"There's none closer than the opposite hemisphere on this continent."

"But they are mind-joining. I can hear them."

"No, listen closely, it is not the same as ours. They are not from Brini-la. They are from *here*."

"But the people here cannot mind-talk. You know that as well as I do. If only it had been so we would have found what we wanted and been home long ago."

"Sh, Jouro. Listen!"

Then the aliens had given me a thought-for-thought description of the conversation Jack and I had had as we walked down by the stream on the hot afternoon we'd climbed up to the lookout. They understood more or less what we said when we talked out loud. Apparently we broadcast telepathic signals even when we weren't meaning to, though they were weak. But when Jack and I had really concentrated on joining our minds so that he could show me the inner cave with the strange fungus on the wall, and then when we discussed how it affected the taste of the water flowing out of the mountain-side, the three aliens were in our minds, sharing the experience.

Back in the exploration vehicle they danced round the energy pillar and pounded each other on the back.

"That's the answer! It has to be."

"Quickly, stop them. Send out a signal, Kenli, you're the strongest. They've got to help us."

"They're not listening. I can't get through. There is nothing in their minds now but tiredness and a desire for food."

"We can't let them go. It's unthinkable."

That evening there was long discussion and much mind-sharing in the exploration vehicle down in the forest. The fungus had to be the source of the missing life-stuff. But it had been clear from their thoughts that, small as the young earth-people were, the entrance to the cave was dangerously narrow.

"We have two options that I can see." Porri put it to the others. "We can blast an opening into the cave..."

"And risk losing our only chance of success in a cave-in," Jouro interrupted.

"Correct. Or we can enlist the help of these young ones."

"Thereby breaking the rule of non-interference."

Porri shrugged. "Do you see a third solution?"

Jouro shook his head.

"We have so little time," Kenli spoke. "These small ones are unique. We may never get another chance. There are no homes up on the mountain, or anywhere nearby. They may leave any time. We must make up our mind without delay."

So they mind-joined and remained so until the plan was complete and agreed upon by all three. They would wait until dark and then lift their vehicle until it was close enough to the plateau to attract the attention of one of the young ones. Then by concentrating their mind patterns they would invite him into their home and use his mind to send a message to the remaining young one, to go into the inner cave, find the strange fungus and bring it to the exploration vehicle. . . .

"We would never have interfered with you were it not for your mind-joinings. We thought you would understand. We did not know you would have such fear of our species. It made it all so difficult." The one they called Porri spoke to me through Jack.

"But why did you take Father?"

"He got caught in the beam. It was too late to switch it off. We regret it deeply."

"Then let him go. Please."

"We can't. Not till we have the fungus and are free to leave. He can't understand. He doesn't mind-join. He would go straight to your authorities. They would threaten our vehicle and we would have to leave empty-handed. I'm sorry. It is only for our protection."

"It will not be for long." It was the softer-sounding thoughts of the one called Jouro. "You understand the urgency of our need. You *will* help us get the fungus?"

"Go through the passage into that cave? I...I can't. I just can't." Even the thought of that narrow crack appalled me. My throat was dry. They felt my panic and for a moment my feelings were so strong that all three minds drew back and I was alone. Then they were with me again, reassuring, persuading.

"We depend on you. Our lives, our whole world. Everything."

"You can do it, Julia. You are strong enough."

"I'm not. Really I'm not."

"Yes, you are. The only thing you're really afraid of is being afraid."

"Face it head on. And you'll find it's nothing."

"I can't. I won't! And you can't make me!"

"We have your father and brother. You will do as we say." Kenli's thoughts became suddenly as sharp and cold as icicles. For a moment I panicked. But I'd been inside their minds as well as they being in mine...

"You won't hurt them. You don't ever hurt people. You'll let them go anyhow!"

Jouro's thoughts were full of laughter and the hardness went out of Kenli's. "You're right, of course. We can't harm them. We can only — ask."

The funny thing was that, as soon as I had called their bluff and I no longer felt I was bargaining for Father's and Jack's life, I wasn't really afraid that much. I remembered with sudden clarity that they had given up Planet Earth and all it had meant to them and gone into exile, just to give us humans a chance to grow up. I really didn't have any choice but to help them in return, did I?

"I'll go now. Tell me what you want me to do."

For a moment the loving warmth of their thoughts was around me like a cloak. And then I was outside the UFO, sitting against the pine tree. Cold, hungry and not nearly as brave as I had felt the instant before...

I was still cold inside, sitting in the blazing sun against the hot rock close to the source of the stream.

Doug had listened to my story without saying a word. Now he looked at me, his face as impassive as ever.

"And that's what it's all been about, all through our history? Strange visitors and flying saucers? Just a dying people looking for a miracle cure!"

"Thank goodness you believe me! Oh, Doug, you can't think how relieved I am. It all sounds so incredible I can't believe it myself."

"I'll tell you what convinced me — that part of the story about them leaving the seed grain of bread-wheat behind as a gift."

"Why that?"

"It's always bothered me...just too much of a coincidence. Listen, Julia. To get bread-wheat you have to cross wild wheat with goat grass. That makes a hybrid called emmer. It must have happened accidentally thousands of times, but the resulting hybrids are usually sterile. *Then* you have to cross emmer with another goat grass to form bread-wheat, and plant geneticists know that that particular hybrid should have been sterile, except for a mutation on one chromosome!"

"And now we know that it wasn't just a lucky accident. Bread-wheat was a laboratory-developed hybrid. It was the Brinians'."

"I always felt it couldn't be chance."

"It was a miracle...but a different kind."

"Yeah. Now you're going to make another one happen."

"By getting them the fungus?"

"If they're right."

"They can't be quite sure until they analyze some of it. But first I've got to go in the cave and get it for them."

"The girl with claustrophobia. You know I'd do it like a shot if I could only get through."

"I know. It's all right. I do have to go, don't I? I mean, there isn't any other way."

Doug said nothing. He looked at me, and my question hung foolishly in the air between us. I stood up and stretched. Down in the valley the trees grew close, hiding the saucer completely. Beyond the trees the smooth round summit of Lookout Mountain shimmered in the sun. Nobody was moving over there either.

"You...you'll come in the cave with me, won't you, Doug?"

"Of course. I'll stay as close to you as I can." He swung the haversack onto his shoulder and began the climb up and along the rocky slope to the west. Coming from this direction and knowing what to look for, it didn't take us long to find the cave entrance.

It was dark and cold inside and there was an icy lump

in the bottom of my stomach even though I was boiling hot from the climb. I took one last longing look at the blue sky and the sun on the mountains. It was so great out there. Wide and open...

Doug got the flashlights out of the haversack and we squeezed in through the entrance of the cave. Inside it was even colder than it had been the day before, and the darkness seemed to be a solid thing, pressing in on me from every side. I could feel the weight of the mountain over my head, hundreds and hundreds of tons of solid rock. It was getting awfully hard to breathe.

"Are you all right, Julia?"

I swallowed. "Oh, Doug, I don't know if I can do it. It was bad enough last time when Jack was here. This time I don't even have him. I can't feel him in my mind at all. I'm alone, Doug."

"The rest of us are that all the time, Julia. You've been luckier than most with this thing you've got with Jack."

I tried to imagine what it would be like, to be always alone inside one's head. To have nobody to share with: those first scary days at a new school, the put-down feeling when kids laughed at a mistake, the happiness of holidays with Mother and Father. It was all so much a part of my life that until recently I'd never thought about being different from other people, except that we had always known somehow that it was not a thing to talk about or show off to the other kids in school. Those two weeks last summer when Jack and Father were down in Cypress Hills were the first time I'd ever felt alone in my whole life, and I'd hardly been able to bear it till he got home. Was that how everybody else felt, all the time?

Doug's face was shadowed above the flashlight, and I couldn't read his expression. "I'm sorry, Doug," I stammered in the dark cave. "I guess I never realised before. I was just being selfish. It must be terrible — not having anybody."

I caught a flash of teeth as he smiled. "Some of my people still have this ability that you and Jack share — not much any more since we've lost our beliefs, but some. It was always good for doing things together, like hunting or having a council. But it was always the custom for each one of us, before he could be recognised as a man and a full member of the tribe, to go away by himself, to be completely alone for three days and three nights."

"Why?"

"To find himself. To find his purpose in life. In order to find yourself you have to learn to be alone. In the old days a boy would go without food or water until the spirit came and showed itself to him."

"Did it always?"

"Yes, always. Then he would live his life by what the spirit showed him."

"I don't understand how it worked."

"I guess really it means that when you are alone with yourself and face your own strengths and weaknesses you can learn how to become a person."

"Doug, I just don't know how to be alone. How to do something difficult without Jack helping me along."

"There's only one way of learning, isn't there, Julia, and that's by doing it."

I stood surrounded by my loneliness in the cave, with the shadows of our flashlights dancing on the walls. I thought about a whole people on some planet far away, slowly dying. I felt as if I were a glass with a small drop of courage in the bottom. If I moved too suddenly it would all be spilt and then there would be nothing.

I looked over at Doug, standing in the shadows. He seemed to know how I felt and he didn't say anything or touch me. He moved his flashlight so that it shone on the crevice in the wall through which I must go, and slowly I walked over to it.

As I edged myself into the crack there was a smell of ancient dust in my nostrils and cold hard rock against my face. The flashlight was almost useless in this narrow space. I could move my right arm up and down in an arc that lit up momentarily the rock walls just ahead of me; but, as the beam from a lighthouse makes the night more noticeable when it has passed, so the darkness around me seemed even more profound. I switched it off after a while and relied on feel.

The sweat was pouring off my face and my hands were so wet I was scared I'd drop the flashlight, yet at the same time I felt as cold as if all the blood was draining out of my body. Suppose I fainted here, in this crevice, I thought in a panic, I could lie wedged in here for ever. Doug couldn't reach me and he couldn't get in touch with Jack. Better to be sensible and get out now while I was still able to.

I got as far as two shuffling steps backwards towards the opening when what Doug had said hit me, like a sniff of smelling salts, jolting the blood back to my head until I could feel my cheeks flame...To be recognised as a man, to be a full member of the tribe, one must be alone, completely alone...

Come on, Julia old girl, I told myself. Time to join the human race. It isn't for long, just ten minutes each way. You've used Jack's courage all your life. Time to do it on your own. It's yours, and no one can take it from you. Ever....

I pushed forward blindly. Something caught my

sweater. I wriggled around and the flashlight slipped from my hand. As I bent towards it there was a ripping sound and I was free again. My hands closed around the flashlight and I switched it on. The glass had cracked but mercifully it still worked.

Now I could see that the sense of freedom I felt was more than just the unsnagging of my sweater. The crack was widening into a sizable passage. I could stand upright and walk forward with my shoulders barely brushing the sides. In another ten steps I was through.

I swept the light around the long cave. It danced off the ceiling, high and hung with stalactites. They were just the way I had seen them through Jack's eyes, like sticks of dirty rock candy. Over to my left the whole wall gleamed wetly. I walked carefully towards it across a floor bumpy with accretions of limestone. The strange bittersweet smell was all around, and faintly I could hear the sound of rushing water.

There was the fungus, greyish-white patches against the dark wet rock. It looked so insignificant, so ordinary. Yet, if the aliens were right, the whole future of Brini-la depended on it. It seemed awfully unlikely... until I remembered penicillin.

I picked at the stuff with my finger-nails. It clung closely to the porous rock, leather-tough and yet paper-thin. How on earth was I going to get it off and into the box. Stupid! Why hadn't I thought it out properly? My knife was in the tent, over on the other mountain. I clawed at the stuff with both hands, but made no impression on it.

The Brinians had given me all I would need, they had told me. Maybe I'd better believe them and stop improvising. I dug in my shirt pocket for the container that had materialised on the grass outside their capsule. It was made of a pearly plastic material, as smooth and warm as wax. I turned it over in my hands. Like the UFO it seemed to have no hinges, no openings, no seams.

Darn it, open, won't you! My fingernails were now in no state to open even a candy wrapper, but suddenly, as I snarled at the thing, a lid, where no lid had been before, slid back. Thought patterns? Could they really do that?

I ran my fingers curiously around the opening. I couldn't even see where the lid had gone to. Ouch! One of the edged was a sharp as a knife. I sucked my finger and then grinned. I finally knew what I was supposed to do.

I held the box under the fungus patch and pushed it gently upward. The sharp end cut through the tough material as if it were butter, and the flakes of fungus fell into the container. I scraped at the wall until the container was full.

Shut! I told it and the lid slid back into place. It was a marvellous toy. I turned it round and round in my hand, now just a pearly white oblong, no bigger than a cigarette pack, with no visible seams.

Then the sense of time came back to me. It was frightening to think that the survival of a whole race might depend on the contents of this little box. I put it in the breast pocket of my shirt and carefully buttoned it down before turning back.

The crevice lay like a dark slit before me. I moved as fast as I dared, terrified of getting snagged or of twisting and ankle on the rough floor, but with a sudden fierce urgency forcing me on. This time my anxiety was not for myself.

I was covered with dust and sweat when I finally wriggled and pushed my way past the last obstinate obstacle. I could see a glimmer of light from the entrance, and I could smell the scent of hot grass. Doug was waiting. He hugged me breathless and then we scrambled outside.

The heat and light were like physical blows after the long clammy dark. I gasped and reeled back into the shadow of the entrance, while Doug wet a handkerchief to wash the dust off my face and hands. He put the canteen down and stiffened suddenly. He rummaged through the haversack for Father's binoculars.

"What is it, Doug? What can you see?"

"Two cars. Parked below Lookout Mountain. RCMP I think. Three...no, four men. Barry must have got Dave Ross to believe him after all!"

He slung the glasses round his neck, threw the haversack over his shoulders and grabbed my hand. "Come on, Julia, we're going to have to run for it, if we're to get to the UFO before they do. Once they put up their defenses you won't be able to get through."

CHAPTER SEVEN

We plunged straight down the smooth rock and the patches of slippery scree in a sort of sideways jogtrot, faster than would have been humanly possible at any other time. If we'd slowed down for a minute or stopped to think where we should put our feet next we'd probably have broken our necks. But somehow the very speed of our descent kept us on our feet, the way a top stays balanced so long as it goes on spinning.

The dust smoked up behind us. I prayed that the RCMP wouldn't pick those moments to look across the valley. We were leaving a signal behind us that could have been seen for miles.

I knew that Doug was counting on the fact that the unfamiliar terrian and a fear of the unknown would slow them down. They were much closer to the UFO, mile for mile, than we were. But they didn't know that, and I'd bet they were scared. We knew just where we were going and why, and *our* only fear was not getting there in time.

We pounded across the rough grass at the foot of the mountain and plunged in among the trees. Doug let go my hand and put up both his arms to protect his face from tree branches, but he didn't slow down for a minute. I followed as fast as I could in his tracks. The pines were all spikes. They seems to whirl past us at a dizzy pace as we ran, their branches reaching out like barbed wire to catch and tear. My sweater got snagged again, I suppose on the same tear I'd made in the cave. I pulled desperately, felt the buttons give and left it hanging on the tree.

The sweat was running into my eyes by now and there was a gasping pain in my right side. Doug seemed to be made of iron or whipcord. Nothing affected him. I couldn't go on another step. There was a blackness behind my eyes darker than the shadows of the trees. I stumbled and went headlong with my face in the stream.

The water poured over me and I let it run into my open mouth. Then Doug's hands were under my arms, hauling me to my feet, and we were across the stream and dodging through the trees again.

The UFO was in sight at last, silver-grey among the dark pines. The defenses were still down. In the blazing afternoon the forest was silent, smelling of resin. The birds and the squirrels slept in the shadows. Way over towards the east I heard a branch crack. We were in time, just.

Together Doug and I stood almost under the rim of the saucer. There was no sign of life from within. Down east I heard a whistle blow. From over to the north came an answering whistle. They'd probably found the trail through the wood. Soon they would be closing in.

I fumbled with the button of my shirt pocket and drew out the precious box. Then I reached out to Jack in my mind. "I've got it, Jacko. It's all right. But they've got to hurry. The police are almost here."

There was an almost inaudible hum and directly above us a door slid open. Standing in green shadow were my father and brother. I saw them through a blur and dazzle of tears as they climbed down onto the rim of the saucer and jumped to the ground.

One of the Brinians stood in the doorway, holding onto the edge with one hand. The other hand reached down to me. I stood on tiptoe to give him the box. As he took it our hands touched. I felt a shiver go through my whole body. We were alike and yet so immeasurably different, from the same world, but evolved a million years apart.

It was Porri. His thanks poured over me, and behind him I could feel the thanks of the other two. I wished that they could have stayed, that we could have got to know each other — as people.

The sun gleamed silver bright on his protective clothing, but as he bent towards me his plastic visor was in shadow and I could see his cat-eyes clearly. They wrinkled at the outer corners as he smiled at me, a very human sort of smile. I smiled back. There just weren't any words. Then he stepped back into the grey-green shadows and the door slid shut and hid him from us. There was a faint humming that grew slowly more intense. I could feel the hair on my arms rise and prickle.

"Run!" Jack shouted suddenly. "Run for the camp. They're taking off!"

We dodged around the glowing exploration vehicle and went north through the trees to the trail leading up to the plateau. Behind us the humming had grown to a swarm of angry mosquitoes. Just as we left the trees we heard a shout behind us. We didn't stop or turn but pounded on up the path to the grassy meadow where we camped.

Our tents stood there. The fireplace lay cold. The

cooking things were still lying around from our hasty breakfast. It all looked amazingly ordinary and peaceful. All out of breath we collapsed on the grass at the very edge of the plateau where we could look down into the forest below without being seen. The humming was growing louder and the glow from the surface of the UFO became so intense that it shimmered among the trees. The RCMP would surely see it now. Not that it mattered any more. They were leaving.

As we watched, the saucer lifted gently from among the pines and spruces, its rim seeming to revolve in a dazzle of coloured lights. It paused for a second above the tree-tops, then shot straight up in the air and spun like a skipped stone over the camp and out of sight beyond the saddle between the two mountains behind us. It was gone in an instant and the shadow of its passing was quicker than a bird's flight.

Down in the valley we could see a pale circle of bent and splintered trees. We were silent, oddly flat now it was all over. Then Father put his arm around my shoulder and I felt close and wonderful. I looked at Jack once and then looked away shyly. The pride and admiration in his eyes were more than I could handle without bawling.

"Shall I light a fire and make tea?" Surprisingly my voice came out normal.

"Good idea," Father approved. "And I'll remind you that Jack and I haven't eaten today, so bear it in mind. I think the two of us had better get out of our pyjamas into something more conventional...we're going to have visitors in a few minutes."

"What'll we tell them? What can we say?" Doug asked.

"They won't believe my story, not possibly," I wailed. "And anyway it's...private."

"We won't tell them a thing, then. You're right. They wouldn't believe the truth if we did tell them. And I think you'll find that they don't really *want* to know anything."

"So we'll just play cool and dumb, eh, Dad?"

"Right, Jack. Least said, soonest mended."

The fire was burning brightly and the kettle was beginning to sing before the policeman's shadow fell across the grass in front of me. I looked up from the peanut butter sandwiches and smiled winsomely. At least it was supposed to be winsome, but it didn't have much effect. The uniformed man continued to stare at me with a pair of the coldest grey eyes I had ever seen. I was suddenly aware of my tangled hair, the scratches on my face and hands, the dust and grime on my runners and jeans. The grey eyes left me and swept over the others, noting Doug almost as dishevelled as me, Jack and Father noticeably cool and tidy in clean shorts and shirts.

Father was marvellous. He had found his old pipe and he was squatting down, lighting it with a splinter from the fire. He looked steadily up at the newcomer as he puffed.

"Yes?" he asked, when it was going to his satisfaction. "Is there anything we can do for you, officer?"

"You saw that...that *thing* that just flew over here?"

"Of course we saw it. We're not blind. It went right over our heads. In my opinion a forest reserve is a most unsuitable place to be testing secret weapons."

Father's voice was quietly disapproving. I was finding it awfully hard not to giggle. I kept my head down over the sandwiches and only looked up when the RCMP officer wasn't looking. He stood stiffly. His hair was cropped, his face expressionless; but I suddenly realised that he was really very young, certainly young enough to recognise the quiet authority in Father's voice and young enough too not to be quite sure how to handle it.

He went on valiantly. "What do you have to say about it?"

"What do *I* have to say? Why, nothing. My dear sir, I'm a school teacher, not an army officer. I suggest that you get in touch with the Defense Research

Board. They may be able to give you an explanation of that extraordinary thing.''

"May I have your name, sir? Identification? And these young persons?''

"My driver's licence.'' Father handed it over.

The man stared at it and then at Father. "You're Mr. Christie?'' He seemed completely taken aback.

"Why, yes. We haven't met before, have we? These are my children, Jack and Julia. One of my students, Doug Smalltree. We are on a field trip in the reserve, studying the geology of the Rocky Mountain foothills.''

"Just the four of you?''

"No.'' Father tamped down the tobacco with his thumb and relit his pipe carefully. "Another of my students, Barry Trevor, is around here somewhere. He should be back by now. Do you know where he is, Doug?''

"No, Mr. Christie. He and Julia and I were together first thing this morning, but he stayed down in the valley when Julia and I went up the mountain for more samples.'' I looked at Doug in admiration. His voice was almost bored. And the funny thing was it was true, every word. He just made it sound so dull.

"I see.'' The officer looked at our scuffed shoes and torn and dusty clothes. "You must have had a rough time on the mountain. What were you and your son doing all day, Mr. Christie?"

"We spent most of the day quietly down in the forest. It's cooler down there. May I ask what is the point of all this?"

"Just a minute, sir. You're sure that's all — you and your son were down in the forest all day?"

"Why yes, I said so."

"This Barry Trevor — you said he was one of your students? Would you give me an idea of his mental stability."

"*Mental* stability? Well, well." Father puffed away. "Oh, I'd say he was a fairly level headed young man. Perhaps somewhat high-strung under stress. Bright people often are, you know, and he's one of my honour students."

The officer seemed at a loss. Father sat on a rock and puffed tranquilly at his pipe. Silence was always a very effective weapon with him.

The RCMP officer suddenly made up his mind. "You see, it's like this, sir. About three hours ago we received a phone call from the lookout station here. Your student Barry Trevor reported that you and your son had been kidnapped by...well...by aliens." He cleared his throat and looked so embarrassed I began to feel sorry for him. "He managed to persuade the man on lookout duty here to phone the ranger station and they got in touch with us. I'm sorry, sir. But his story was really very circumstantial."

I glanced sideways at Doug. His face was completely impassive. I don't know how he did it. Behind the policeman Jack was just about breaking up. I looked away before he could give me the giggles and busied myself stacking the huge pile of sandwiches onto a plate and making the tea. The kettle had been boiling its head off for quite long enough.

"Can we offer you a cup of tea, officer? Or a peanut butter sandwich."

He shuddered faintly. "Er, no thank you, Miss. Not while I'm on duty."

"I hope you don't mind if we go ahead. I'm absolutely starving, aren't you, Jack?" I sent him a secret look. I knew he'd had his eyes glued to the food ever since I started to prepare it. Now he reached over and grabbed.

The RCMP officer walked to the edge of the plateau and raised a hand in a signal. There was a movement down among the trees.

"Good heavens, are there more of you?" Father peered over his glasses. "Are you quite certain you won't stay for lunch, I'm sure we have enough. Julia, do we have enough?"

"Of course, Father, masses."

"No, no." The poor young man was getting desperate. "Thank you. We can't stay. I have to make my report. Mr. Christie, I just don't know what to say. The whole thing is obviously a hoax, so now there is the question of pressing charges for committing a public mischief."

"Surely not, officer. It could have been a quite genuine misunderstanding. Or it is possible that Barry got a little too much sun yesterday. It was the first day we were out in the field. Couldn't you bind him over to me? He is my responsibility during this trip. I am sure that public mischief would be the last thing he would think of."

"Yes, I think that would be all right, Mr. Christie. I have your address. I'll have to file a report, of course. And I can't promise that charges won't be brought against the boy, but I don't think it's very likely. Just keep an eye on him from now on."

"Oh, I will, officer, I will."

"Then I'll turn him over to your care." He walked rapidly down the path to where the other policemen and the ranger were waiting, Barry among them. He was arguing. He looked hot, angry and bewildered. The other men just looked hot and angry. The young officer took Barry's arm and escorted him firmly up the slope and delivered him to Father like a reluctant parcel.

"Thank you, sir. You do understand that you are personally responsible for his behaviour as long as you're on this trip?"

"Yes, indeed. I'll look after him. Thank you, officer."

The man had hardly turned away before Barry boiled over. "What the...!"

Quick as a flash Doug's hand was over his mouth. It seemed to be his destiny to muzzle Barry. Father smiled faintly.

"Sit down, Barry. Yes, right there. Now, Julia's going to give you a cup of tea and a sandwich, and you are going to eat and drink and not say *one word* until those men are safely out of earshot. Understood?" Barry nodded. "All right, Doug, you can let him go."

Doug released him and Barry sat down sulkily and took the sandwich and mug I held out to him.

"Gosh, I was starving," said Jack, with his mouth full. "Terrific sandwiches, Julia. Hits the spot."

"They certainly are." Father's voice was muffled too. "I never before appreciated the flavour of peanut butter. Julia, my dear, can you squeeze another cup of tea out of that pot?"

While we ate Doug squatted at the edge of the

plateau and raked the valley with the binoculars. I noticed how craftily he shaded them with his hand so that they would send no tell-tale glare to any watching eye. The last thing we wanted when everything had gone so well was to have them think we were interested in anything except food.

"It's okay." He got up and stretched. "They're in their cars. They're leaving."

"I wonder what Dave Ross thinks about all this."

"Who knows. But he'll never say a word. Scared of losing a good summer job."

"I don't think anyone will say another word. I think that particular report will get lost somewhere between desks."

"Mr. Christie, why didn't you tell them the truth? You made them think I was a complete idiot." Barry's pale face was pinched with anger.

"It wasn't difficult," I couldn't help putting in.

"Be quiet, Julia. The truth, Barry? You don't even know what the truth is. You ran away from it."

"But you deliberately *lied* to them."

"No, Barry, I did not. I certainly intended to mislead, but I didn't lie. I merely reinforced what that young man desperately wanted to hear, that we weren't being invaded from outer space."

"That's quibbling and you know it."

"Now listen to me, young man. If you had paid attention to Julia in the first place we wouldn't have got in this mess...RCMP indeed!"

"What had she to do with it? She's only a girl."

Father smiled. "I must caution you, my budding scientist, never to let your prejudices blind you like this. Julia was the key to the whole situation. It was her courage and endurance that brought a happy conclusion to what could well have been total tragedy,"

"Hear, hear," Jack chimed in. "Julia, you were terrific!"

"Doug was a great help. I couldn't have done it without him."

"Well, then, I'm sorry." Barry's voice was almost inaudible. "You might at least tell me what it was all about and how you two escaped from the UFO."

So we sat by the fire and finished our late lunch and talked. The afternoon was warm and my eyes grew heavier by the moment. I let the others do most of the talking. Doug made far too much of what I had done.

"If you knew what I was thinking when I went through that horrible crevice you wouldn't call me brave," I put in when he'd gone on quite long enough. "I wouldn't do it again for a million dollars. Anyway, now I'm so sleepy I can't keep my eyes open."

"Let's all have a snooze till supper. It's been some day."

We wandered off to our tents. I was glad of the chance to be alone with Father. Jack and I could get together any time, alone or in a crowd, but with Father it was harder to be private. I slipped off my filthy jeans and shirt and lay down on top of my sleeping bag. It was cool and shady in the tent and heaven to be lying down.

"Father, were you scared in the UFO?" I asked abruptly.

"You bet I was. But after they'd explained everything to you the Brinians let Jack and me wander round. Jack was able to explain some of their ideas to me. Fascinating. Absolutely fascinating."

"I'm so glad you're safe."

"So am I, my dear child. I'm even gladder for you. You're gained something really special out of this day, haven't you?"

"Does it show that much?"

"It does to me. I used to worry about you sometimes — my little worrier, the tag-along twin. But not any more. You've grown up and become a person all on your own, haven't you?"

"Do you know, I believe you're right. I guess I saw my spirit clearly, the way Doug said. Now I know what it is to be me, and I don't have to hold onto Jack any more the way I used to, because I was too scared to be me. And now I *am* me, we still have each other, only more than ever. Does that make any sense...?"

I could feel my voice trailing off and I wanted to say something else important but I was too sleepy to remember what it was.

Chapter Eight

When I woke up the inside of the tent was pitch dark. For a moment I thought I was back two nights ago, before any of it had began. Had it after all been just a dream? But the new sure feeling inside told me differently. It had been real, the whole incredible adventure.

I heard Jack talking to the others outside. "She's awake now."

I rummaged in my kit for a clean pair of jeans and a sweater, pushed my feet into moccasins and lifted the tent flap. The eastern sky was already dark, but when I went out I could see that behind the western mountains a pale green reminder of the day lingered on. There was a huge fire going, sending cheerful sparks up on the still evening air. There was a big pot at the edge of the fire. It smelt wonderful and I said so, yawning and stretching luxuriously. I felt as if I'd been asleep for a hundred years and wakened up to a magic new world in which everything was clearer and brighter and spicier.

"It's only canned stew. But there's potatoes and corn baking in the embers. Combined male effort. A salute to our Julia."

"Thanks, guys. That's terrific. I'm sorry I slept so long."

"You woke up just in time. Grab a plate and we'll start."

We sat on the grass by the fire looking down across the valley. The stew was spicy and rich and its gravy was great with the baked potatoes. We had the corn as a separate course, in our fingers, with dollops of butter. I guess we were really hungry, and that's why we didn't notice it at first, not until the shadow of it blotted out the stars directly above us.

"It's them. They're back!" Jack spoke softly, and we all stared up at the shadow hovering above our heads.

"What do they want now?" Barry shied away like a spooked horse. He still didn't understand them. Maybe he couldn't. The rest of us didn't answer. We just watched in silence as the saucer settled, gently, like a butterfly on a flower, till it hovered only a few inches above the grass beside us. There were no lights, no eerie glow, no prickly sense of power. Just a shadow at dusk.

Then a wonderful sense of peace and thankfulness swept over me. I reached out to Jack's mind and found it there too. Impulsively I caught Father and Doug by the hand, and at the same instant Jack reached out to Barry and Father. Maybe the Brinians were strong enough to make the sharing work. I emptied my mind and let the feeling flow through me into the others.

...Our thanks go beyond words. It is as we hoped. The fungus is the answer to the sickness of Brini-la. Now we can go home. The search is over. To you who made it possible we leave a gift and the knowledge that what you did for us will never be forgotten, so that if we ever meet again, here or on Brini-la, it will be in honour and friendship. Farewell...

The shadow moved. The saucer skimmed across the grass, dislodging a stone which clattered down the slope towards the trees. It glowed green, the rim flashed brightly. The silence was broken by a hum that rose to a piercing whine. Then, like a stone from a sling, the UFO leapt straight up, up and out into the night sky.

"Goodbye. Safe voyage," I whispered after it.

We looked up at the sky for a long time. It was silly, really. There was nothing to see up there but the stars.

The gifts the Brinians promised us? We never spoke about them to each other, but I can guess.

Jack's telepathic powers and mine are much greater now, strong enough even to help other people, though we try to remember the Brinian way of non-interference.

Father has been working on a new magnetic force theory, from what he picked up on his tour of the UFO. Most evenings he and a mathematician friend work on the details. They're getting very excited about it and think they're on the verge of a break-through which should change the world energy situation for the better.

There has been a new look in Doug's eyes since that night on the mountain. He is as gentle and considerate as ever, but he has become more forceful and sure of himself. I imagine that one day he may become a great Indian leader.

Barry? Well, maybe it was just coincidence, but the next morning going down the trail he tripped over a hunk of rock that hadn't been there the day before. It turned out to be a nugget of almost pure gold, a geological absurdity, Father said. Barry didn't care. The way he grabbed it you could tell he'd got his heart's desire.

I got an extra gift, which seemed unfair, as the others were just as much a part of it all. The second gift? It doesn't sound like much. I'm not afraid any more...of being lonely...of new things...of fear itself. It doesn't sound like much. But to me it is the best gift of all.